LOST

IN THE MOUNTAINS OF DEATH

WARNING!

The instructions in this book are for extreme survival situations only. Always proceed with caution, and ask an adult to supervise - or, ideally, seek professional help. If in doubt, consult a responsible adult.

Published 2014 by
A & C Black, an imprint of
Bloomsbury Publishing Plc
50 Bedford Square, London, WC1B 3DP

www.bloomsbury.com

Bloomsbury is a registered trademark of Bloomsbury Publishing Plc

ISBN 978-1-4729-0621-2

Text copyright © 2014 Tracey Turner
Illustration copyright © 2014 Nelson Evergreen
Copyright © 2014 A & C Black
Additional images © Shutterstock

Printed by CPI Group (UK) Ltd, Croydon CR0 4YY

1 3 5 7 9 10 8 6 4 2

MIX
Paper from
responsible sources
FSC
www.fsc.org   FSC® C020471

LOST

IN THE MOUNTAINS OF DEATH

TRACEY TURNER

A & C BLACK
AN IMPRINT OF BLOOMSBURY
LONDON NEW DELHI NEW YORK SYDNEY

5

South America

VENEZUELA

Caracas · Port-of-Spain

★ Georgetown
GUYANA · Paramaribo
SURINAME · Cayenne
FRENCH GUIANA

ATLANTIC OCEAN

★ Bogota
COLOMBIA

Quito ★
ECUADOR

PERU

★ Lima

The Andes mountains

★ La Paz
BOLIVIA

The Atacama Desert

BRAZIL

Brasilia ★

PARAGUAY

Asuncion ★

PACIFIC OCEAN

CHILE

Santiago ★

URUGUAY

Buenos Aires ★ · Montevideo

ARGENTINA

SOUTH ATLANTIC OCEAN

★ Stanley
FALKLAND ISLANDS

Tierra del Fugeo

Welcome to your adventure!
STOP! Read this first!

Welcome to an action-packed adventure in which you take the starring role!

You're about to enter the Patagonian Andes, a dizzying landscape of tall peaks, icy glaciers and howling winds. On each page choose from different options – according to your instincts, knowledge and intelligence – and make your own path through the mountains to safety.

You decide . . .
- How to escape an attacking puma
- How to survive an avalanche
- How to avoid disaster on glaciers and frozen lakes

. . . and many more life-or-death dilemmas. Along the way you'll discover the facts you need to help you survive.

It's time to test your survival skills – or die trying!

Your adventure starts on page 7.

Something ice cold splashes onto your face and you wake with a start. You blink water from your eyes, sit up and look out across a sparkling mountain landscape covered in freshly fallen snow. You're lying between some rocks, with your backpack covering you. It's cold, but you're wearing warm layers.

It takes you a moment to remember where you are and what's happened. You were trekking with friends in the Andes, South America's spectacular mountain range, when an unseasonal snowstorm blew up and now you have been separated from the rest of your group. You look at your watch. It's eleven o'clock – the storm blew up hours ago! You must have banged your head and passed out. You're lucky to be alive.

You stand up and shout for your friends. Your voice echoes around the tall peaks that surround you. You strain your ears for a reply, but there isn't one. You try again anyway. Nothing, except the drip of melting snow. High above you in the clear blue sky a condor circles. You are completely lost. And entirely alone.

In your backpack you have a number of useful things: crampons (to attach to your shoes so you can walk on ice); two thermal foil blankets; a container for boiling water; matches in a waterproof container; a couple of spare thermal T-shirts; a Swiss army knife; a trowel; and a torch. You hoist your backpack onto your back and with no other option set off into the mountains.

How will you survive?

Turn to page 8 to find information you need to help you survive.

The Andes mountain range is the longest in the world, stretching more than 7,000 kilometres along the western coast of South America. It stretches from the tropical rainforest in Venezuela, on the northern coast of South America, to the southernmost tip of Chile. The Andes mountains are the highest in the world outside of Asia. It's a vast and inhospitable environment and many people have become lost in the Andes, never to return. If you're going to survive you'll need to have your wits about you.

Patagonian Andes

You are in the Patagonian Andes, around a million square kilometres of spectacular scenery, with high mountains, glaciers and sparkling lakes. You came at the very beginning of the trekking season, which runs from November to April (summer in the southern hemisphere), but the weather here can be unpredictable and changeable, and you've been unlucky. Patagonia is a region, not a country, at the southern tip of South America, shared by the countries of Chile and Argentina.

Perils of the Andes

The temperature, with cold winds and the possibility of more snowstorms, is one of the perils you will have to contend with. Others are pumas, altitude sickness, steep drops, difficult terrain, avalanches and earthquakes, to which the area is prone.

Extreme Andes

The Andes span seven countries: Venezuela, Columbia, Ecuador, Peru, Bolivia, Chile and Argentina. Because the Andes cover such a vast distance, and because the mountains are so high, the Andes mountain range is a land of extremes.

• The 'cloud-forests' of the Andes are found in the tropical north, where the warm air of the rainforest meets the cold air high in the mountains, and causes clouds to form.

• The Atacama Desert, in northern Chile, is one of the driest places on Earth, and the highest desert in the world.

• The Andes are on the Pacific Ring of Fire (see page 37), which causes earthquakes, volcanoes and also hot springs and geysers.

• There are hundreds of thermal springs in the Andes caused by the volcanic activity. El Tatio is a geyser field high up in the Andes with more than 80 active geysers. It's the largest geyser field in the southern hemisphere.

• The Tierra del Fuego is the world's most southerly place where people live permanently. (People visit and stay in Antarctica, but they don't live there all the time.) The Tierra del Fuego is made up of one large island and lots of smaller ones.

Turn to page 10.

Mountain Survival Tips

Here are a few basic tips that might affect your chances of survival in the mountains . . .

- The right clothes are vitally important in cold weather. Wear layers of clothing: the layer next to your skin should be able to keep moisture away from your body, the next layer should be warm, and the outer layer should be wind- and waterproof. Fortunately, you are warmly dressed, and you're wearing a hat, gloves, and sturdy walking boots.

- Make sure you know how to start a fire and practise before you set out on a trip somewhere cold. It could save your life. (Find out more about fire building on page 87.)

- If you get wet, take off your clothes and dry them and yourself before putting them back on. The water will make your body temperature drop very quickly, and even if the temperature seems quite mild you'll be in danger of hypothermia.

- Don't try to climb steep inclines without the proper equipment and expertise.

- Making a shelter when you're not walking should be a priority. Look at pages 15 and 71 for more on shelter building.

Turn to page 11.

You've been walking some time when huge, grey clouds come racing over the tops of the mountains. They cover the sun, and soon there's no sign of the blue sky any more. As the air turns colder, your heart sinks: another storm must be on the way. Should you set off in the hope of finding your friends? Or stop and make shelter?

If you decide to walk, go to page 24.

If you decide to make shelter, go to page 14.

It gets more difficult to walk, until each step takes a huge effort. It doesn't look like it, but perhaps the slope is steeper here. Your head is still pounding– in fact it seems to be getting worse and you're starting to feel sick as well.

You think you've probably caught some kind of bug. Perhaps the best thing to do is find somewhere to stop and rest? Or maybe it would be better to head for lower ground?

If you decide to find somewhere to rest, go to page 22.

If you decide to change direction and head for lower ground, go to page 44.

Slowly and carefully, you walk towards the rocks where you thought you heard the noise. As you round a large boulder, you find out what caused it. You are staring into the yellow eyes of a large puma.

You feel sweat break out on your forehead and swallow hard. The animal is big and muscular. It hasn't taken its eyes off you and its ears are flattened against its head. You figure that this probably isn't a good sign. In fact it's difficult to see anything good about this situation. The puma is only a few metres away from you – just a couple of large bounds of its powerful legs and it would be on top of you.

What should you do?

If you decide to curl into a ball and play dead, go to page 38.

If you decide to back off, go to page 27.

The clouds look as though they could burst with snow at any moment, and the wind howls around you in icy gusts. You look around for something to help make a shelter with before the storm arrives.

There are some rocks and boulders that you could shelter behind, using your blankets as covering, which would make a very hasty shelter. There's also a small wood a bit further down the slope – you could shelter in the trees.

If you opt for a hasty shelter in the rocks, go to page 45.

If you choose to make for the trees, go to page 35.

Shelter Building

Which type of shelter you build depends on the conditions – how much time you have to build it (if it's getting dark you'll have to be quick), how cold it is, or if there are dangerous wild animals about. Here are some general tips.

• If you're on high ground make for somewhere lower down so that you're not so exposed to the wind. Very low ground might be prone to flooding, frost and mist, so avoid that as well.

• Forest shelters are fairly easy to make and the tree canopy will also provide shelter from the elements. But be careful of falling branches.

• If there's a thunderstorm, beware of sheltering under trees, which may attract lightning.

• Even a shallow depression in the ground will give you some protection – if it's raining, though, it will soon turn into a muddy puddle. If you're on a flat plain and a storm blows up, your only choice might be to sit with your back to the wind and pile your equipment around you.

• More permanent shelters can be made by forming walls from logs (piled between two parallel rows of upright sticks) or stones (but be very careful with this – they could collapse). But you'll need plenty of time to make a more sophisticated shelter.

The storm is getting worse and the snow stings your face as the wind hurls it about in strong, icy flurries. You're starting to shiver, and you're sure finding shelter is the right thing to do. But you don't know how long the storm is going to last and how long you'll be stuck here. Which type of shelter should you build?

You could simply find a spot sheltered by rocks and use your backpack and blankets as extra cover. This will only take a few moments.

Or you could construct a better shelter by finding a big boulder and digging out a trench behind it, on the side facing away from the wind. Then you could build another wall around you out of large stones, and snuggle down in the trench with your backpack and blankets over you.

> If you decide to make a very basic shelter in the rocks, go to page 45.

> If you decide to find a boulder and start digging a trench, go to page 26.

You know that the most important thing is to stop the bleeding, so you grab a spare T-shirt from your backpack and press it to the wound. After a few moments, the blood stops flowing. You tear the T-shirt into strips and make a bandage, which you tie firmly around your wound but not too tightly.

You sit down on a rock, have a drink of water and feel much better. Something catches your eye – in the distance are some yellowy-white blobs, and eventually you realise that they're sheep. You can just about make out a fence, keeping them in. A sheep farm must mean farmers!

You set off towards the fence.

Go to page 114.

The next bit is a bit steep, and it's extremely windy up here. But you're determined to get to the next ridge – you'll have a condor's-eye view from there, and it's not very far away.

You remember that you should have both hands and one foot secure before you move the other foot, and you make sure that your hand-holds and the foot-hold for your left foot all feel comfortable and safe. You look down to see where the next foot-hold is for your right foot, and swing your leg up to get to it. But as you do so, your left foot slips, and you lose your hand-holds too. Panic-stricken, you scramble desperately for another firm grip, but it's no good – you plummet downwards, knocking your head as you fall.

The end.

Mountain Climbing

- You should never attempt to climb a mountain without proper gear (see below), training, experience and expert knowledge. No wonder you fell! You shouldn't climb alone, either – you need other climbers for back-up and safety.

- As well as all of the above, you'll need to make quick decisions and judgements which could mean the difference between life and death. So make sure you are alert and calm, have a clear head, and aren't in danger of panicking.

- You need to be fit and strong – climbing mountains is physically demanding.

- Essential mountain-climbing gear includes a climbing helmet, ropes, harness, carabiners (which connect ropes together safely), ice axe, ice hammer, and climbing boots.

You were sure the blizzard would have blown over by now, but it's still howling around your ears and battering you with tiny icy snowflakes. You are shivering violently and very tired, and decide to sit down and wait out the storm.

The snow makes it difficult to see, and you feel very confused. Was it really just today you were walking with your friends? You struggle to remember. As you stagger over to a boulder and sit down, you realise you've stopped shivering. You feel exhausted but, strangely, you feel quite warm now and unzip your jacket. You slump sideways and fall asleep.

You have severe hypothermia. Unfortunately, you don't wake up.

The end.

Hypothermia

Doctors divide hypothermia into three phases:

- If you're body temperature has fallen to between 32 and 35 degrees Celsius, you have mild hypothermia. Symptoms include shivering, tiredness and rapid breathing.

- You develop moderate hypothermia if your body temperature drops to 28 to 32 degrees Celsius, and symptoms include confusion and irrational behaviour, difficulty moving, shallow breathing and slurred speech. You will probably stop shivering – but this is definitely not a good sign.

- You have severe hypothermia when your body temperature is below 28 degrees Celsius. Your pulse becomes weak, pupils dilate, and you will probably pass out. Even with medical attention, people in this stage of hypothermia might die. Without it, they certainly will.

You're feeling worse than before, and now you have a nasty cough as well. Maybe you'll feel better after a rest.

You sit down protected from the wind by some rocks. You take everything out of your backpack, put the blankets around your shoulders, and lay everything else out around you in a semicircle. Somewhere at the back of your brain you know this is an odd thing to do, but you decide not to worry about it.

Resting isn't going to make any difference to what's wrong with you. You have altitude sickness, and there's a cure for it: descending to lower ground. If you don't, symptoms could get worse, and you could end up with swelling in your brain or a build-up of fluid in your lungs, both of which can be fatal. As you sit and rest, your symptoms become worse. You start to hallucinate, before falling into a coma. You're dead within 24 hours.

The end.

Altitude Sickness

- People react to high altitudes differently – you were unlucky to experience altitude sickness, which can be treated by descending to lower ground. It's quite rare for altitude sickness to develop into high altitude cerebral oedema (in which fluid builds up around the brain), or high altitude pulmonary oedema (a build-up of fluid in the lungs), but when it does it's often fatal.

- Early warning symptoms of altitude sickness are a headache, tiredness and nausea. If you don't descend to lower ground, these symptoms will become worse, your heart might start to pound, and you might feel dizzy.

- Severe symptoms include breathlessness and coughing. People sometimes become very clumsy, and behave irrationally – which definitely isn't helpful when you're halfway up a mountain.

Even without the sun and blue sky, the landscape is beautiful. If you weren't lost and alone, you'd be enjoying the trek and the scenery. You're surrounded by snow-capped mountains, and here and there in the distance you can see lakes and smooth, blue-white glaciers.

The clouds continue to build as you walk, rolling over the mountain tops, and the wind gets stronger.

Go to page 42.

Andes Climate

- The Andes stretch all the way from the top of South America to the bottom, so the climate varies massively. In the north of the country, the climate is tropical, but the Andes are so high that they are still cold. Almost all of the world's tropical glaciers are found in the Andes. The southern part of the mountain range is much colder.

- The Andes mountains are a barrier between the Pacific Ocean and the South American continent: to the west of the central Andes the climate is very dry, and the eastern plains of Argentina also have extremely dry weather.

- You are in the Patagonian Andes, towards the south of the continent, between Chile and Argentina. The weather is famously changeable here, and it's prone to sudden storms (as you've found out).

You start digging with your trowel. The ground is very hard, but you're determined, and finally succeed in making a shallow depression just about big enough to lie down in. The wind is stronger now, and the snow finds its way inside your jacket, making you wet as well as cold. You're chilled to the bone.

You're shivering, so you open your backpack to pull out a blanket, but it's instantly whipped out of your hand by the wind, and goes flying off into the distance. You take out the other blanket and wrap that around your shoulders. Teeth chattering, and feeling weak and exhausted, you go and sit down behind the boulder, abandoning your plans to make a shelter.

You are in the early stages of hypothermia. The blanket isn't enough to warm you up in this blizzard, especially since your clothes are damp. Soon, you fall unconscious.

The end.

You inch backwards, slowly, keeping your movements calm and controlled even though your heart is pounding wildly. The big cat is still staring in your direction, but it no longer seems ready to spring.

You step back further and keep still. The puma flicks its ears, then turns and bounds away, moving fast. You breathe a long sigh of relief as you watch it. Soon the animal is out of sight.

Go to page 30.

You don't have much further to go before you find it: a fast-flowing stream, which must be fed by meltwater from the mountain.

You are pretty sure that this water will be safe to drink, but you make a fire (see page 87 for more on making fires) and boil it anyway. You're already lost, and you don't want to risk getting sick as well.

You drink some of the water once it's cooled a bit, and the hot drink – even though it's just water – makes you feel a bit better. The crackling fire is good for your spirits too. Once you've filled your water bottle, you put out the fire carefully.

Go to page 58.

Water Needs

- Even in cold weather, you still need to drink over a litre of water per day to replace what you lose by breathing and sweating – more if you're doing hard work. If you don't, you're in danger of dehydration, which can kill you. Luckily, there's plenty of water in the Andes.

- It's always a good idea to boil water, even from a clear mountain stream like this one – there could be a dead animal in it further upstream out of sight.

- You could also melt ice or snow to drink. But don't eat snow without melting it first – if you're already cold, eating snow will make you even colder. And don't eat crushed ice, which could injure your mouth.

The sun has come out, and the tall peaks of the Andes look even more dramatic against the blue sky, but you're feeling jumpy and too nervous to enjoy the scenery. You realise there are lots of dangers in this remote part of the world.

Maybe you should stay here, where it seems relatively safe, rather than risk rockfalls, avalanches, steep drops and dangerous wildlife if you keep travelling?

If you decide to keep going, go to page 74.

If you decide to stay put and await rescue, go to page 98.

You scramble up the mountainside, dislodging a scattering of small rocks as you go. It's steeper than it looked, and more difficult. You don't have any climbing gear, but you're not planning to climb up vertical cliffs. Even so, perhaps you should find an easier route?

If you decide to climb back down and find a less difficult path, go to page 46.

If you decide to continue climbing, go to page 18.

The ground shakes beneath your feet again. You squat down, and an even more violent tremor almost makes you lose your balance. You're very glad you're not near anything that could topple down on you – the rocks and boulders from the mountainside, for example.

Earthquakes are not uncommon here: the Andes are on the Pacific Ring of Fire, where the plates that make up the Earth's crust meet and collide with one another (for more on earthquakes, go to page 37).

The ground stops shaking. You're aware that there could be another quake at any time, but you can't stay here forever, you need to keep moving. A quick movement catches your eye – scuttling away from the mountainside there's a small grey furry shape – a chinchilla. Maybe it was disturbed by the tremor.

Watching the animal scurry into the distance, you take out your water bottle, but it's empty. You're thirsty, and look around for a water source. There's snow higher up on the mountain – you could make a fire and melt some. Or you could go in search of a stream.

If you decide to melt snow, go to page 50.

If you decide to find a stream, go to page 89.

Chinchillas

- You were lucky to see a chinchilla – they're rare animals in the wild, and they're usually active at dawn and dusk.

- Chinchillas can measure up to about 30 centimetres long. In the wild, they live only in the Andes in Peru and Chile in groups of up to 100 animals.

- Because they're prey animals (predators include eagles, pumas and foxes), chinchillas have evolved the clever trick of shedding a clump of fur, leaving the animal unharmed, if they're grabbed.

- They're very agile, and can jump up to 1.8 metres high.

- Chinchillas are rare partly because of their very soft, warm coats, which meant they were hunted for their fur.

The clouds roll away across the mountains and the sun shines on the fresh snow. It's starting to melt already.

You're distracted from the spectacular view by a terrible headache. You feel tired, too, even though you've just had a rest. You're feeling a bit sick as well.

This would be a terrible time to fall ill. But you don't feel that bad, you tell yourself. Maybe you should just keep going and hope you feel better soon? On the other hand, you've heard that being high up can make you sick. Perhaps you should head for lower ground.

If you decide to head for lower ground, go to page 44.

If you decide to keep going as you are, go to page 12.

You shelter under a bent tree. After an hour or so the wind starts to die down. Soon the snow stops, and the air feels a little warmer. You crawl out from underneath the tree and make your way to the edge of the wood.

You look out across a wide valley, beautiful in the fresh snow. You can see quite a long way, but there are no signs of life. Optimistically, you call out for your friends again – but all you hear in reply is the echo of your own voice.

You wonder if you should climb up higher – perhaps with a good view you'll be able to spot the rest of your group?

If you decide to climb, go to page 31.

If you decide not to, go to page 34.

The ground trembles again, this time more strongly, and small stones come skittering down the rocks.

You're beginning to wonder whether you should have taken cover when suddenly the ground rocks violently, knocking you off your feet. You hit the ground hard and as you struggle to get up, the sound of crashing and tumbling makes you look up: huge boulders are crashing down the mountainside, dislodged by the earthquake. Unfortunately, you are right in their path and there's nothing you can do to get out of the way.

The end.

Earthquakes

- The Earth's crust is made up of enormous 'tectonic' plates, which move and grind against one another constantly. When two plates grind together and one gives way, it causes an earthquake.

- The border between the Pacific plate and other large tectonic plates lies around the edge of the Pacific Ocean. An arc around the Pacific – stretching from New Zealand, through New Guinea, the Philippines and Japan and across the Pacific Ocean to the western coasts of North and South America – is known as the Pacific Ring of Fire. Not surprisingly, it's very prone to earthquakes.

- Most of the world's earthquakes are very minor. But big ones can cause large numbers of casualties and terrible damage, as buildings topple and cracks open up in the earth.

- Millions of years ago, the colliding tectonic plates of the Pacific Ring of Fire caused the Andes mountains to form.

- Volcanoes are also common around the Pacific Ring of Fire – 75% of the world's earthquakes, both active and dormant, are found here. The highest volcanoes in the world are in the Andes – the highest is Ojos del Salado on the Chile-Argentina border, which is almost 6,900 metres high.

You have made a fatal mistake. Pumas are opportunistic predators and if they see the chance of an easy kill, they will take it. When you were standing up, the puma was probably just as worried about you as you were about it, but now that you've curled up into a ball, defenceless and vulnerable, it sees you as easy prey.

The animal is powerful and fast. It's only a matter of seconds before it's all over.

The end.

Puma

- Pumas are also known as mountain lions, cougars, and catamounts. They're solitary animals, and very shy, so they're rarely seen.

- These animals are large and powerful. They weigh up to about 60 kilograms, with a head and body up to about 1.5 metres plus an extra 70 centimetres or so for the tail.

- Pumas are found in North and South America, from Canada down to the Andes in southern Chile. They once roamed the whole of the United States, but now they're only found on the west coast, apart from the endangered Florida panther (which is a type of puma despite its name).

- These big cats prey on animals as large as deer and vicunas, and in this part of the Andes they also prey on guanacos and south Andean deer, as well as smaller prey such as hares. They usually kill by delivering a fatal bite to the back of the neck - so at least it's over quickly for you.

- If they've made a big kill, pumas will keep it hidden and return to it over a few days.

- Pumas do attack people, though very rarely, usually a person out hiking on their own.

It gets darker as the night draws in, and you turn on your torch. The tiny patch of ground it lights up only makes you feel more vulnerable. It's cold too – you can't move fast enough to keep yourself warm because of the darkness. You're beginning to wish you'd stopped to build a shelter, but it's going to be tricky to do that in the darkness.

Just as you decide to stop and find somewhere to sleep for the night, you slip and plummet down a steep slope you hadn't realised was there. In a few seconds, it's all over.

The end.

The Andes' Highest Peaks

- The Andes mountain range is second only to the Himalayas and its associated ranges for the world's highest mountains.

- Aconcagua in Argentina is the highest Andes mountain, at 6,962 metres.

- The second highest, Ojos del Salado, is also the highest active volcano in the world (although it hasn't properly erupted since around AD 700). It's on the border between Chile and Argentina, overlooking the Atacama Desert, one of the driest places on Earth.

- Although Aconcagua is the highest peak, it's not the most difficult climb. Mount Fitzroy, in the Patagonian Andes in Chile (also known as Cerro Chalten) is only 3,375 metres, less than half as high as Aconcagua, yet it's a notoriously hard climb because of its sheer rock faces. Only very experienced climbers attempt it.

- Chimborazo is the highest mountain in Ecuador at 6,268 metres and lies on the Equator. Even though there are taller mountains, its peak is the farthest point on the Earth's surface from the centre of the Earth. This is because of the equatorial bulge – there's a bulge at the Equator, caused by the Earth's rotation, of 42.72 kilometres.

The wind bites viciously and the snow stings your face. Maybe it would be better to stop and find some kind of shelter – if you can in these conditions.

If you decide to stop and find shelter, go to page 16.

If you decide to brave the blizzard, go to page 20.

Y ou fit into the cave quite snugly. You take out
your thermal blankets and wrap them around you.
Protected from the wind, you feel much warmer.

The sun has nearly set, and it's getting colder. It would be
lovely to have a fire to keep you warm, and perhaps make a
hot drink. But would it be worth the effort?

If you decide to make a
fire, go to page 86.

If you decide not to bother and go to
sleep in your shelter, go to page 80.

You do start to feel better now that you're on lower ground. It's easier to breathe, and you don't feel so tired or sick. You were experiencing mild altitude sickness, which affects some people at higher altitudes and can develop into a life-threatening condition if you don't descend to lower ground. Find out more about altitude sickness on page 23.

You think you spot a movement in the rocks ahead of you – something big. Should you go and investigate, or stay away in case it's a dangerous animal?

If you decide to investigate the movement, go to page 13.

If you decide to walk in a different direction, go to page 30.

Your shelter is very basic, but it protects you from the snow and the extremely fierce wind. All you have to do now is stay as warm as you can under your blankets, and wait out the blizzard.

It's not long before the wind stops howling, and things sound much calmer. After a little longer, you're sure the storm is over, and you stick your head outside. The clouds are moving swiftly away, and you can make out a watery sun behind them.

Go to page 34.

You scramble back down the rocks. Looking up, you can see it was too difficult a climb to attempt without proper climbing gear, and anyway you probably wouldn't be able to see your friends if they can't hear you when you shout. You shout again, just in case. There's still no reply.

You walk along flatter ground. You feel fine, apart from a nagging headache.

Go to page 34.

You were taking a bit of a chance by heading for the trees, but luckily it doesn't take long to reach them, and there's still some light left. One of them is a huge conifer, and its branches reach all the way to the ground. You peer inside – it's like a ready-made tent. You're protected from the wind and you even have a soft carpet of pine needles to sleep on.

It would be lovely to have a fire to keep you warm, and perhaps make a hot drink. But is it worth the effort?

If you decide to make a fire, go to page 86.

If you decide not to bother and go to sleep in your shelter, go to page 80.

You step onto the snow with a crunch. It seems pretty easy to walk on, and the wind does seem a bit less fierce this way. As you trudge across the slope, you hear a 'thunking' sound. You wonder what it could be – maybe there's someone walking higher up? You call out.

The 'thunking' sound is followed by a rumble, and then cracks appear in the snow. You freeze, then turn and make a run for it. But you're too late. The snow cracks up and starts to slide downhill, taking you with it. You're hurtled downhill with the snow, and buried under a thick layer, which sets rock-hard within moments.

The end.

Avalanches

- There are usually warning signs that an avalanche is likely – in this case, the recent earth tremor was a sign that you should stay away from areas where an avalanche could occur.

- After an avalanche the snow sets as hard as cement within seconds, making it impossible to move or breathe. You won't be able to dig yourself out once the avalanche has stopped, unless you're very near the surface.

- There are two types of avalanche: a loose snow avalanche is made up of powdery snow, and isn't usually dangerous; a slab avalanche is when big chunks of heavy snow break away from a layer of snow underneath them, and is very dangerous. Snow in a slab avalanche can hurtle down a mountainside at 130 kilometres per hour.

- If there's a heavy snowfall, the fresh snow can make the layer of snow underneath it unstable. Avalanche warnings are issued under these conditions.

- Most avalanches are caused by the weight of a skier, snowboarder or snowmobile on snow that's unstable.

It's a bit of a climb up to where there's still snow on the mountain. You make your way carefully, choosing a path that means you can walk upright, without needing to use your hands to climb. You realise that would be extremely dangerous, even though there's a much quicker route to where the snow is. You don't want to risk a fall, which you know would spell your doom.

It's cold and windy here, and you make a fire as quickly as you can in the shelter of some rocks (see page 87 for more on making a fire). You melt snow in your container, drink some and melt more to fill your bottle. Then you carefully put out the fire and carry on.

Go to page 58.

Dangerous Mountains

Mountain climbing can be fun and exhilarating, but it can also be very dangerous. The world's most dangerous mountains to climb include:

- Mont Blanc is in the Alps, on the border between France and Italy. It's popular with climbers, but has claimed thousands of lives.

- Only 191 people have tried to climb Annapurna in the Himalayas, which is over 8,000 metres high. Sixty-one of them have died trying.

- More than 700 people a year now reach the summit of Mount Everest, the world's tallest mountain at 8,848 metres. Hundreds have died in the attempt since the first person reached the summit in 1953.

- Mount Fitzroy in the Patagonian Andes is a difficult climb, with sheer granite faces. Its isolated position means that few people try to climb it – roughly one person per year.

You rummage in your backpack for something to make into a pair of gloves (or at least mittens), and come up with an old thermal T-shirt.

Before you start, you make sure your bootlaces are securely tied. You rip the T-shirt in half, and wind the material around one hand, making sure you can still move your fingers about, then secure it with an elastic band. It's trickier doing the same to the other hand, but you manage it with the help of your teeth. It's going to be difficult tying your shoelaces from now on, but at least your hands are warm.

Go to page 76.

The dawn light wakes you up and you peer out of your shelter. You're still completely lost and have absolutely no idea which direction is best. You look at the landscape and decide which way to go. You could either climb a gentle slope and walk along higher ground, or go down a slightly steeper slope to lower ground.

If you decide to head for higher ground, go to page 72.

If you decide walking on lower ground would be better, go to page 64.

There's a roaring noise behind you. You spin around, and suddenly you're very glad that you moved away from the snow – it's rushing down the mountain in an avalanche. You stand and watch for a while, until the snow stops moving and silence descends again. The snow has built up into a huge drift: if you were buried underneath it, the chances of getting out alive seem slim. Thank goodness you decided not to walk across the snow.

The sun's beginning to go down. Soon it will be twilight. Maybe you should build a shelter for the night?

If you decide to build a shelter, go to page 70.

If you decide to carry on, go to page 40.

Surviving an Avalanche

- If you're going skiing or snowboarding, always check for avalanche warnings before you leave. If you can't get avalanche reports, don't head for the slopes after a heavy snowfall (which could destabilise the snow underneath it), or if there have been earth tremors.

- If you're caught in an avalanche, try to keep hold of a ski pole, if you have one. You can poke it out of the snow to alert rescuers, as long as you're near enough to the surface.

- Take off your skis, they'll only make things worse.

- Always carry a transceiver, which will tell rescuers where you are.

- As the avalanche draws to a stop, try to make an air space in front of your face by vigorously punching at the snow – it will set hard very quickly.

- Don't shout out unless you're sure rescuers are close by, otherwise you'll be wasting precious air.

You shoo the birds away, take some of the meat and make a small fire (see page 87). You use a sharp stick to act as a spit, reasoning that the heat will kill any bacteria that might be present. When it's cooked you tuck in hungrily.

But soon you bitterly regret having eaten the meat. As you continue on your way, you start to feel pains in your stomach. An hour or so later, you begin to vomit. Then the diarrhoea starts . . . things are not looking good.

You retch violently, feeling weak and sick. You know that without a supply of clean water to replace the fluids you're losing, you'll dehydrate. You dig the blankets out of your backpack and slump against a rock. You don't have the energy to make a proper shelter, and as the night draws in, you die of hypothermia (see page 21).

The end.

Food Poisoning

- Food poisoning can be caused by bacteria (which is what happened in this case – the meat wasn't freshly killed), or a virus. It causes vomiting and diarrhoea and can last for several days.

- Food poisoning can be caused by not cooking or storing food properly, or food can become contaminated from a person (or animal) touching it with dirty hands (or claws/beak!).

- Foods that are especially prone to causing food poisoning are raw meat, eggs, shellfish and ready-prepared foods such as sandwiches.

- Symptoms of food poisoning usually start a day or so after eating the contaminated food, but some types can make the victim ill almost straight away – in these cases, vomiting is the main symptom.

- Usually, victims of food poisoning don't need medical attention: as long as they drink plenty of water and rest, they recover.

- Without drinking water, the victim can become dehydrated, which is potentially fatal.

Ahead of you stretches a flat, white sloping plain of thick snow. Maybe the blizzard was worse here, or perhaps the snow has never melted here because it's in the shadow of the mountain that towers above you, pointing craggy peaks into the brilliant blue sky. Maybe you should walk across the snow? Your boots are waterproof, and it looks as though it's easy going.

If you decide to change direction and head away from the snow, go to page 54.

If you decide to trudge across the snowy slope, go to page 48.

You run to the stream. The blood is pouring from your wounded hand and you're feeling the energy draining out of your body as it flows.

You plunge your hand into the stream – it's ice cold, which only makes the blood flow more freely, and it chills you to the bone. To make matters worse, you get your clothes wet in your rush to put your hand in the water. Your teeth start to chatter.

Feeling weak from blood loss, you slump down next to a tree by the stream. The bleeding begins to lessen, but with no one around to help you, your body temperature drops until you become hypothermic.

The end.

Y ou trudge along, feeling very tired. At least your improvised gloves are keeping your hands warm.

Snow-capped mountains soar around you, and the sun is out, but you're finding it very difficult to keep your spirits up. The mountains just remind you of how small you are, and how vast and remote this landscape is.

Go to page 112.

From your high vantage point, the landscape sweeps down into wooded valleys. Sunlight glints on a distant lake. Snowy mountain peaks stretch into the distance.

You're finding it difficult to appreciate the lovely scenery though, because of a thumping headache. You're a bit out of breath, too – maybe because you're travelling uphill. Perhaps you should travel on lower ground?

If you decide to keep going on higher ground, go to page 79.

If you decide to turn back and travel on lower ground, go to page 64.

You can see the blue lake glittering below you, and you're still wondering whether it might make a better route. But just then, there's a scuffling sound above you that makes you look up. On the rocks, just out of reach above your head, is a small furry animal. It's a guinea pig!

You know that in this part of the world it's common to eat guinea pigs, in fact people breed them for eating. You're feeling very hungry. Maybe you should go after the guinea pig, catch and roast it? After all, you won't get very far if you become too weak.

If you decide to go after the creature, go to page 108.

If you decide to keep going, go to page 96.

Cautiously you put one foot onto the ice, pressing down to make sure it doesn't crack or move. It seems to be safe, and you let the ice take your full weight. The surface of the ice looks solid, and you can't hear any cracking sounds. Crossing the lake here will save you lots of time. You walk out onto the ice, taking careful, sliding steps.

It's not long, though, before the ice does start to crack. You try to race back the way you came, but you're too late. The ice breaks, and you plunge into the icy lake. You don't have time to haul yourself out before hypothermia sets in. You struggle out of the ice-cold water, and just about make it to the bank. But by this time you're too confused and disoriented to get warm and dry and save yourself.

The end.

There are two condors circling in the sky, getting lower and lower. One of them swoops down – it looks as though it's landed just on the other side of a rocky outcrop. Slowly, so as not to alarm the bird, you step around the rocks. Only a few metres away from you, there are three of the large birds feasting on something – it looks as though it could be a dead guanaco. Another condor swoops down to join the others in their meal.

The birds are surprisingly ugly close up, with bald heads and hooked beaks. One of them spots you and gives an alarmed cry, hopping backwards from the carrion with its massive wings outstretched. The condor's wingspan looks twice your height! The bird cocks its head to look at you, then hops back to the dead animal.

Hunger gnaws at your stomach. Should you chase away the condors and eat some of the meat yourself?

If you decide to eat some of the meat, go to page 56.

If you decide to leave the condors to their feast, go to page 73.

Andean Condors

- Andean condors are some of the world's biggest flying birds. They weigh up to about 15 kilograms and have a huge wingspan of up to 3.2 metres. Although the wandering albatross has a wider wingspan, Andean condors' wings are the largest of any bird.

- Because they're so large, even that wide wingspan needs a bit of help, so the condors live in areas where there are high winds and they can surf air currents without having to flap their wings.

- Andean condors are black, with a white collar around the necks of the male birds. They have bald heads, similar to other vultures.

- Like all vultures, condors feed mainly on carrion, though they sometimes raid other birds' nests for eggs or newly hatched chicks.

- Andean condors are endangered – there are only a few thousand of them left.

You've never walked on a glacier before, but it looks simple enough. You strap on your crampons and head out onto the ice. It's more difficult than you'd thought, and it takes you a while to get used to walking on the spikes of your crampons. You learn, after slipping over, that you have to put your feet flat onto the surface of the ice. It's quite tiring.

You're getting the hang of it and making good progress when something catastrophic happens: the layer of snow you're walking on suddenly gives way and you tumble into a crevasse. You hit your head and die instantly.

The end.

Crevasses

- Crevasses are cracks in a glacier or ice sheet. They can be up to 20 metres across, 45 metres deep, and hundreds of metres long.

- Crevasses can be impossible to see under a bridge of snow, which may not be thick enough to take a person's weight. They can catch out even the most experienced climbers.

- Because of the danger of crevasses, it's important for trekkers to rope themselves together – that way, if someone does fall into a crevasse, they can be pulled out by the rest of the group.

- Anyone planning to travel on a glacier should take special training in crevasse-rescue techniques.

- Glaciers are moving rivers of ice, so new crevasses open up all the time, and old ones close.

You hardly notice the dangerous drop and loose rocks surrounding you because you're so intent on your quarry. There it was again! A brown-ish, furry shape disappears into some rocks above you. There's a short climb to get to where it vanished, and you fearlessly haul yourself up, hand over hand, flailing about for footholds with your feet.

Once you've made the climb, though, you find yourself on a perilously narrow ledge. For the first time you realise the seriousness of your predicament: you are perched on a thin ledge with a drop of about 20 metres below you. There is no sign of the guinea pig. A gust of wind scours the ledge, nearly sweeping you off it.

You gulp, and start to climb down. Climbing without the correct gear in a strong wind is, of course, highly dangerous. You manage about a metre before you slip and fall.

The end.

Guinea Pigs

- Guinea pigs are descended from wild rodents called cavies, which are very slightly different, and one of which has just spelled your doom.

- The animals are native to South America, where guinea pigs are bred for food. They breed easily and don't take up much room, so they're a very popular source of protein. Guinea pigs were first domesticated around 3,000 years ago.

- In North America and Europe, guinea pigs are kept as pets. There's evidence that they were kept as pets as far back as the 1500s in Europe, after the Spanish Conquistadors brought the animals back from the newly discovered New World.

- Cavies also have bigger relatives. One of them is the capybara, the world's biggest rodent, which looks like a giant guinea pig and is also from South America. Another is the mara, which looks more like a large hare or a jackrabbit.

In the gathering dusk, there isn't much time for building a shelter. You spot a small opening in the rocks close by, which might mean you don't have to bother. You take a closer look: it's a small, dark cave. It doesn't look very cosy, but it would offer protection from the wind.

Or maybe you should go in search of a different shelter? There are some trees in the distance, and you think it should only take you half an hour or so to reach them.

If you decide to shelter in the cave, go to page 43.

If you decide to walk to the trees, go to page 47.

Shelter

- Unless you're somewhere very hot and low on water, shelter should be your first priority in a survival situation. In very cold conditions, you won't last long without protection from the weather.

- Use whatever materials are to hand to make your shelter. On a snow-covered mountainside with no trees, it's possible to make a shelter from the snow itself, by cutting it into blocks. People who live in the Arctic all year round sometimes construct shelters from turf.

- Try not to get your clothing wet in very cold conditions. You might work up a sweat building a shelter, so before you start your hard work, take off the layer of clothing closest to your skin, leaving on a waterproof layer, and replace it when you've finished your hard work and can dry yourself off. Or wear a material that keeps moisture away from your body.

- Whatever type of shelter you have, make sure it's ventilated. If it isn't, you'll die.

- Wet clothes can be left outside your shelter overnight – they'll freeze, and in the morning you can shake off the ice.

The wind feels colder the higher you go, and the going is difficult. You huff and puff as you climb the steep slope. You begin to wish you'd done a bit more training before setting off on the trek.

Go to page 61.

You watch the condors for a bit longer before continuing on your way. You skirt around the birds so as not to disturb them, and you're far enough away from them that they look up and watch you but don't leave their meal. One of them watches you for a while with something long, red and slimy sticking out of its beak.

Go to page 88.

You have a sudden strange sensation as you walk – it feels as though the ground's vibrating slightly. Above you, a few small stones come skittering down the mountainside. The last of the stones bounce down, and everything is quiet again.

It must have been a very minor earthquake – you remember hearing that the area is prone to them. Maybe, to be on the safe side, you should change direction and find somewhere to walk that isn't near possible falling rocks? On the other hand, it was a very small vibration, and the shaking's completely stopped now – it might be better to just carry on your way.

If you decide to find somewhere away from the mountainside, go to page 32.

If you decide to carry on as you are, go to page 36.

However cold the temperature, it's always best to take off wet clothing and get dry.

You begin to shiver uncontrollably in your wet clothes, and your teeth start chattering. You sit down to rest on a rock, and notice that you've stopped shivering. Maybe this is a good sign? But then you start to feel confused. You look around you: how did you get here? Anyway, it doesn't matter because you feel very tired and decide to lie down and go to sleep.

You have hypothermia (see page 21 for more information), and never wake up.

The end.

You spot a movement from the corner of your eye: in the distance, you make out a group of eight small deer.

These are South Andean deer, which only live in this part of the world. They're rare, so you're lucky to see them.

The animals haven't caught sight of you — you must be downwind of them. They start to move off calmly, and you wonder if you should follow them. They might lead you to water, and you need to fill up your water bottle.

If you decide to follow the deer go to page 83.

If you decide not to follow them, go to page 60.

South Andean Deer

- South Andean deer, or huemul, are the national symbol of Chile and appear on the Chilean coat of arms.

- The animals are small – about 80 centimetres tall – and brown or brownish grey in colour.

- They are only found in the Andes in southern Chile and Argentina.

- Their numbers have reduced drastically in the last 100 or so years and they're now in serious danger of becoming extinct.

- The deer are preyed on by pumas and foxes, but habitat loss is their greatest threat.

You put your hands under your armpits as you walk to keep them warm. But when you need to tie your bootlace, your fingers get very cold very quickly. Maybe you should stop to try and make some gloves?

If you decide to make something to keep your hands warm, go to page 52.

If you decide to keep going as you are, go to page 84.

The wind whistles around your ears. Despite the fact that you're walking as fast as you can, you're absolutely freezing. Your headache is worse – a searing pain behind your eyes – and you're finding it even more difficult to breathe. Wearily, you sit down and drink some water. It takes an enormous effort to get up again.

You really should have turned back. You stop and rest, but don't get any further. A mixture of altitude sickness (see page 23), exhaustion and hypothermia (see page 21) combine to kill you.

The end.

You crawl into your shelter feeling extremely tired. Night falls, and you're quickly asleep.

During the night, the temperature drops as cooler air sweeps down from the mountains. Your body temperature drops so much that, as you sleep, you develop hypothermia. You wake up, but when you do you're too tired and confused to take any action. You go to sleep again, and this time you don't wake up.

The end.

Fire for Survival

- Fire is the most important element for survival in cold conditions. As well as keeping you warm – which is vital to keep you alive in colder climates – a fire cheers you up, and makes you feel like you are in control. This is an important factor for survival when you're lost and alone.

- A fire should create warmth that will continue for most of the night – heated stones will carry on giving off heat for hours.

- A fire means you can cook food and boil water to make it fit for drinking. It can also be used to dry damp clothes.

- You can use small stones from the fire to dry out boots – drop them into your boots using two sticks. Hot sand can also be used – shovel it up in a metal container. But check that the insides of the boots aren't burning.

- However, bear in mind that fires can also be extremely dangerous. Make sure you're not in danger of starting a forest fire, and that you can light it, contain it, and put it out again safely.

You're soaked from the knees down. You take off your wet trousers, socks and shoes, hopping from foot to foot to try and keep warm. At least you don't feel any colder without your wet clothes, but you're still absolutely freezing. You pull a spare T-shirt out of your backpack and rub your wet skin vigorously until you're dry. Then you wrap yourself up in a blanket and gather the makings of a fire. This isn't easy with the blanket wrapped around the bottom of your legs and feet, but luckily you don't have to go far to find some bark for tinder, twigs for kindling, and bigger twigs for the fire. (See page 87 for how to make a fire.)

Once the fire is burning, you put your boots, socks and trousers out to dry, and take the opportunity to have a rest. You take two sturdy twigs, pick up hot stones from next to the fire, and drop them into your boots to dry them out. You soon feel warm again. By the time your clothes and boots are dry, you're feeling fine.

Go to page 109.

By the time you arrive, the animals have moved on but you were right in thinking they might lead to water and discover a small shallow pond where they had been grazing. Sunlight glints on the surface of the water. It looks clear and clean.

It would take time and energy to make a fire, and you're very thirsty. You know that the water in the Andes is famous for being pure and safe to drink. Also, the water must be clean enough for the animals to drink. So maybe it's not worth the bother of boiling it?

If you make a fire and drink boiled water, go to page 60.

If you decide not to bother and drink the water anyway, go to page 106.

You keep walking, warming your hands under your armpits as you go. Often you need to use your hands to keep your balance or to tie a bootlace, and they start to get cold.

Eventually, when dusk begins to fall, you need to make a shelter and fire for the night. But without gloves, your hands soon become numb. You succeed in putting a shelter together, but your hands are too shaky to make a fire. You manage to get to sleep, but your body temperature drops too much during the night. You become hypothermic and die.

The end.

Frostbite

- It's important to keep your hands warm – when you need to do something to help you survive, such as make a fire, numb hands will prevent you.

- In colder conditions, below minus one degrees Celsius, fingers and toes can be prone to frostbite – this is when skin and tissues freeze.

- White or waxy-looking fingers, or tingling and numbness, can be early signs of frostbite. Fingers should be warmed up by placing them under your armpits or in warm, but not hot, water.

- Never rub frostbitten fingers or toes – this causes more damage.

- Very severe cases of frostbite need surgery or even amputation.

Luckily you've practised lighting fires many times before your trip to the mountains, so you know how to do it safely and efficiently. You gather together some bark, small twigs and logs. Your matches have survived undamaged and dry, and you light one first time, sheltering it from the wind. Soon you have a healthy fire going inside a ring of stones, which will give off heat later on when the fire's died down.

You hold out your hands to the fire, feeling pleased with yourself and optimistic about a good night's sleep tonight, and finding rescue tomorrow. You heat up some water over the fire and drink it hot, which makes you feel warmer still. You go to sleep snug and dry.

Go to page 53.

Making a Fire

- Before you start, gather together everything you'll need: a prepared fireplace, matches, tinder, kindling and fuel.

- Choose a fireplace that's sheltered and dry.

- Set your tinder alight – this is very dry, flammable material, such as powdered bark, cotton wool, or the inside of a bird's nest. Good tinder will only need a spark to light it.

- Build your kindling around the tinder in a pyramid. Kindling is small, dry twigs that will burn quickly and easily.

- Gradually add larger pieces of wood, taking care not to add anything too big or too wet in the early stages, or you'll put the fire out.

- If there are stones available, place them in a circle around your fire. The stones will heat up and give off warmth after the fire has gone out, and they'll also stop the fire from spreading out of control. But be careful not to use very wet stones, which can explode!

You nearly trip over one of your bootlaces – they've come undone on both boots. You take off your gloves to tie them, crouching down with your back to a sudden strong gust of wind.

When you've finished, you turn to pick up the gloves from the rock. But they're not where you left them. The wind must have blown them off the rock! You start searching. Unfortunately, though, you're just in time to see one of them flying off down a very steep slope, far too dangerous for you to follow. The other glove is lying on the ground not far away, but as you reach it the wind catches that, too, and whirls it over the precipice after the first one.

Does it matter that you've lost the gloves? Should you spend time and energy working out how to make some new ones? The weather's cold, but these aren't Arctic conditions.

If you decide to try and make some new gloves, go to page 52.

If you decide not to bother, go to page 78.

You're really thirsty now, and you know there must be a stream around here somewhere – there's no shortage of water in the Andes. There's a lush green forest ahead of you, and you think you can hear the sound of running water, though the high, buffeting wind makes it difficult to tell.

You carry on, heading towards the source of the sound.

Go to page 28.

Your stomach growls again. But you decide it's better to be hungry than risk eating a plant you're not completely sure about, and you're not feeling too weak yet.

You sense you're being watched and spin around. You have to squint to see it, but sitting on some rocks staring at you, is a grey animal, well camouflaged against the rocks. It looks like a fox. You decide not to disturb it, but while you're looking at the fox you're not watching where you're putting your feet. You stumble over a big stone, fall and badly gash your hand on a sharp rock.

Blood is pouring from the deep wound. What should you do?

If you decide to bandage the wound, go to page 17.

If you decide to wash it in a nearby stream, go to page 59.

Patagonian Fox

- The animal you've seen is a Patagonian fox, or South American grey fox, which are native to Patagonia and western Argentina.

- These small predators weigh up to about 4.5 kilos, and prey on rodents. They also eat berries, birds' eggs and insects, and scavenge carrion or pumas' leftovers.

- The foxes' favourite food, hares, aren't native to Patagonia, but were introduced from Europe in the 1800s.

- Patagonian foxes help one another out. Female foxes that don't have cubs share their food with other female foxes and their cubs. This cooperative behaviour helps the species survive.

You walk downhill across rocky terrain to the lake, sparkling in the sunshine. Close to the shore there's a beautiful sight: a flock of Chilean flamingos, bright pink against the blue water, feeding in shallow water.

Keeping your distance from the birds so as not to scare them off, you make a fire at the lake to boil water, then fill your water bottle. The feeding birds remind you that the lake is probably full of food – the birds eat snails and aquatic insects, but there are bound to be fish here too. Your stomach rumbles at the thought. Should you stop and fish? Some food would make you feel a lot better.

If you decide to fish in the lake, go to page 100.

If you decide not to, go to page 94.

Patagonian Lakes

- The Patagonian Andes are scattered with brilliant blue lakes. An area known as the Lakes District includes 20 or so large lakes, which were carved into the landscape during the last ice age. It's the greenest part of Patagonia, covered in temperate rainforests.

- General Carrera Lake in Patagonia is South America's deepest lake. It has a maximum depth of around 590 metres, and is roughly 200 kilometres long, with an area of nearly 1000 square kilometres. Beautiful marble cliffs rise at the edges of the lake, which have been sculpted into amazing shapes and caves.

- Lake Viedma is fed by the Viedma Glacier, which flows into the lake in a spectacular two-kilometre-wide terminus at the western edge of the lake.

- Chilean flamingos, a large flamingo species, are found in Patagonian lakes, especially the saltwater ones. You might also see striking black-necked swans.

You spot a small herd of brown, slender, llama-like animals grazing not far away. They have very long necks, and you're close enough to see their huge brown eyes. They spot you and stampede away at top speed – you're sorry to see the beautiful creatures go. But they've left a thoughtful gift – some of their fleecy hair is stuck to the dry, scrubby bushes dotted about, and you collect some for insulation, in case you need to spend another night in the wilderness.

There's a cheeping noise close by and you spin around. Not far away there's a big bird – it looks like an ostrich with dull grey-brown feathers, about a metre tall. Running alongside the bird are three of its chicks.

The birds are obviously flightless. Maybe you could grab a chick and roast it? You are starting to feel weak with hunger by this point.

If you decide to chase one of the chicks, go to page 110.

If you decide to keep away from the birds and carry on your way go to page 103.

Guanacos

- The animals you spotted are guanacos, which live in South America from southern Peru to Argentina and Chile. They can be found quite high up into the Andes mountains – up to about 4,000 metres.

- Guanacos and their close relatives vicunas are wild animals. Llamas and alpacas are domesticated, bred from their wild relatives. All of these animals are related to camels.

- Guanacos have amazing coats – a coarse top coat and a very soft undercoat. Alpacas are bred for their fleeces, but guanaco fleece is even more soft and luxurious, though they don't have as much of it as alpacas do.

- The animals live in groups of up to ten females with their young and a single male. Groups of young male guanacos can be much bigger, before they leave the herd and go in search of their own group of females.

A blue-white glacier stretches below you. In your bag there are some crampons, which are spiked overshoes so that you can walk on ice and densely packed snow. You have them with you because you'd planned to walk on a glacier as part of your trek. It might even have been this glacier.

Glacier walking must be fun, if people regularly do it on treks. It looks smooth and easy to walk on. Maybe you should put on your crampons and walk on the glacier?

If you decide to walk on the glacier, go to page 66.

If you decide not to, go to page 102.

Glaciers

- A glacier is a river of ice. They move slowly, though usually they don't look as though they're moving at all, but they're flowing like rivers in very slow motion.

- Some glaciers flow faster than others. The record goes to the Kutiah Glacier in Pakistan, which was clocked racing along at 112 metres per day.

- A glacier begins to be formed when snow doesn't melt and more snow falls on top. Thick layers of snow are squashed into ice.

- There are different types of glacier. Ice sheets are the biggest, covering thousands of square kilometres. They're only found in Greenland and Antarctica. Ice shelves are ice sheets that float on the sea. There are various other types too, including mountain glaciers.

- Ten per cent of the Earth's surface is covered by glacial ice. Amazingly, it stores 75% of all the world's fresh water.

- The biggest expanse of glacial ice outside polar regions is found in southern Patagonia. There are 19 large glaciers, and the Campo de Hielo Sur (Southern Patagonian Ice Field) measures around 320 kilometres from north to south.

You spend some time finding a good place to stop and make camp. You choose a site that's near a stream, on flat ground but not in a valley, which might get flooded. It's nice and sheltered here, with a wood nearby where you can find firewood and logs to make a shelter.

You've got time to spend, so you make a really good, sturdy shelter using lots of tree branches. You even find some fleecy hair stuck on some bushes, which you think has come from a guanaco (see page 95), and use as insulation for your improvised sleeping bag. You build a fire pit and get a good fire burning (see page 87 for making a fire). Then you spell out SOS in enormous letters with rocks. You catch fish from the stream, using a stick you whittle into a spear, and you've plenty of water to drink.

You have to wait a week before you hear the reassuring sound of helicopter rotors in the distance. Your heart pounding, you make sure there's nothing covering your SOS letters, and throw some green wood onto the fire to make smoke. The helicopter pilot sees you! You're soon taken to safety, and reunited with your friends.

But you can't help wondering if it might have been a better adventure to keep going.

The end.

You make your way around the edge of the lake. It's longer this way, and you have to negotiate large boulders by the lake side. But you don't fancy your chances on that ice – if it were to break and you fell in, you'd almost certainly die of hypothermia. You take your time, clambering over the boulders carefully so as not to risk getting injured.

Go to page 114.

You decide that your best chance of catching a fish will be to make a spear and lie on the bank and wait for a passing fish. The water is clear, and you don't have any bait for a hook anyway.

But as you approach the edge of the lake, you slip on a slippery rock and plunge feet first into the lake. The lake is fed by a glacier and it is so icy cold that it takes your breath away. You struggle out of the water – only your feet and part of your legs have got wet, but even so it leaves you gasping from the shock of the cold water.

What should you do? Can you bear to take off your boots and clothes and dry them? Or is the thought of exposing your freezing legs to the elements too much to even consider?

If you decide to take off your clothes and get dry, go to page 82.

If you decide to keep walking and dry out that way, go to page 75.

Fishing

- The lake is full of fish – among the ones that are good to eat are perch, which are native to this part of the world, and salmon and trout, which have been introduced here from North America.

- In order to hide from the fish, make sure your shadow doesn't fall on the surface of the water.

- If you don't have any luck spearing a fish with a sharpened stick, you could try making a trap. Use a plastic bottle with the top section cut off, turned around and placed back inside the bottle so that the bottle top is facing inwards into the bottom of the bottle. Fish can swim in through the narrow neck, but will find it very difficult to get out again.

- The biggest danger when fishing here is the cold water. As you've just found out, the waters of a glacier-fed lake are freezing cold.

The glacier looks easy to walk on, but you worry about falling into a crevasse, or slipping despite your crampons, since you're not used to walking in them. So you decide instead to head down towards the lake.

Go to page 92.

As you carry on your way you notice that this side of the lake is frozen because it's in the shadow of a high mountain. On the other side of the lake, maybe a hundred metres away from you, you catch sight of something moving fast. You strain your eyes to see. It's a hare, darting between the rocks as if it's running away from something. You spot the predator: an eagle, ready to swoop.

But as you move your eyes from the eagle back down to the ground, you notice something else. It looks as though there's a fence running along the other side of the lake. And on the other side of the fence, you can now make out some yellowish-white shapes. They're sheep! It must be a sheep farm – which means there must be people looking after the sheep, not too far away!

Although it's not too far across to the other side of the lake, to walk around the lake would take ages – it's several times that distance and covered in boulders. The ice looks solid. Should you walk across the frozen lake, or go around the outside?

If you decide to walk across the lake, go to page 63.

If you decide to walk around the lake, go to page 99.

You decide to cook some of the stems and green leaves, which you hope will give you some much needed energy. You make a fire, boil a little water, add the plant and cook it for a few minutes. It doesn't taste very nice, but you eat hungrily anyway.

You were right – you did indeed read about this plant in a book before you set off on your Andes trek. Unfortunately, it wasn't in the Edible Plant section. This plant is Brugmansia sanguinea, or Blood-red Angel's Trumpet, and it's sometimes eaten in order to fall into a trance and have visions as part of a religious ritual. You start to feel queasy and sit down. Your eyelids feel heavy . . . you fall into a strange waking sleep and dream you've turned into an alpaca. There's no one to look after you and keep you warm. Although the amount of the plant you've eaten wouldn't normally kill you, it keeps you in a trance long enough that you become too cold and develop hypothermia. You never wake up from your strange dream.

The end.

Angel's Trumpet

- Blood-red Angel's Trumpet is native to the Andes, and grows in Bolivia, Columbia, Ecuador, Peru and Chile.

- The plant can grow to about five metres tall. It has thin, oval leaves and huge trumpet-shaped flowers around 20 centimetres long, which dangle downwards from the stems. The flowers can be pink to dark red, and there's a very similar plant, the Golden Angel's Trumpet which has fragrant white or yellow flowers.

- Some Andean people use the plant in rituals to communicate with the spirit world.

- The plant is also used by tribespeople as a medicine to cure a wide variety of problems: rheumatism, arthritis, sore throats, stomach aches, and to clean wounds.

Animals aren't known for their hygiene, and water holes can easily become contaminated. Unfortunately, that's what's happened here. Boiling water will usually be enough to kill germs, but for some reason you haven't bothered. Oh dear.

You carry on your way, but soon you start to feel feverish and sick. You vomit, but it doesn't make you feel any better. You try to struggle on, but keep having to stop – you now have diarrhoea as well. You lie down. There's no one around to help you, and you don't have enough water and salt with you to replace the fluids you've lost. This is the end of the road for you.

The end.

Waterborne Disease

There's a wide and horrible variety of diseases that can be transmitted in water. Here are some to look out for.

- Cholera – spread by bacteria, cholera causes severe diarrhoea. The disease can kill quickly if it's not treated.

- Dysentery – there are two types, one caused by bacteria and the other by parasites, but both cause vomiting and diarrhoea. If the parasitic type of dysentery – amoebic dysentery – isn't treated, it can kill you.

- Typhoid fever – spread by an infected person's faeces in drinking water, typhoid causes fever, sweating and sometimes diarrhoea, and can be fatal.

- There are lots of others – parasites that live in your intestines, viruses that can cause all sorts of horrible symptoms. In a survival situation, always boil water before you drink it.

Your foot slips as you scramble after the little creature. It's scurrying higher up, amongst some boulders. You lose sight of the guinea pig, but you reason that you're bound to come across the creature, or one of its friends and relatives, if you carry on. On the other hand, maybe you should admit defeat. You're hungry, but are you hungry enough?

If you decide to stop looking for the guinea pig, go to page 113.

If you decide to keep climbing, go to page 68.

Your stomach rumbles. You haven't had a meal for ages, and you're desperately hungry. You might start to feel weak if you don't find something to eat soon.

You spot a plant you think you recognise – beautiful trumpet-shaped red flowers hang from a small tree. You are sure you saw the plant in a book about the Andes that you were reading before you started your trek. That probably means it's one of the plants that's safe to eat.

If you decide to eat some of the plant, go to page 104.

If you decide not to eat it, go to page 90.

You don't think the adult bird has spotted you. You creep towards it and its chicks slowly and carefully.

Suddenly the bird sees you. It throws out its flightless wings and screeches. You freeze. The bird is still agitated and the chicks are cheeping frantically. Then the adult bird charges at you, moving incredibly fast. You take off, running as fast as your legs can carry you. In your panic, you trip over a boulder, bang your head and knock yourself out. With no one around to look after you, you die.

The end.

Rheas

- These birds are Darwin's rheas, or lesser rheas. There's also another type, the greater rhea.

- Adult Darwin's rheas can be up to a metre tall. Amazingly, they can run at up to 60 kilometres per hour.

- The birds are often found close to herds of guanacos or vicunas, usually in groups of between five and thirty birds.

- Unusually for birds, male rheas incubate the eggs, which hatch about 40 days after they've been laid, and care for the young birds for a further few months. Male rheas can be aggressive during the breeding season and when incubating or rearing young.

- The famous scientist Charles Darwin discovered Darwin's rheas. The group he was with shot and started to eat one of the birds before Darwin realised it was an unrecorded species, and salvaged part of it to study!

As you round a rocky outcrop, you spot a bright blue lake below you. It's big, and surrounded by boulders and scrubby grassland. There might be fish in the lake, and it would be a good chance to fill up your water bottle.

You think it will take an hour or so to walk down to the lake. Should you change direction and go to the lake, or carry on the way you're going?

If you decide to walk towards the lake, go to page 92.

If you decide to keep going as you are, go to page 62.

You're still hungry, but you think you can keep your strength up enough to keep going. You know that water is far more important than food – you can survive for weeks without it. And anyway, you're bound to be rescued soon.

You look at the sky hopefully, imagining a rescue helicopter or a plane, but all you can see are two condors against the blue sky.

You have to pick your way through large stones and boulders, which is tiring. But you keep going, telling yourself that everything will be all right.

Go to page 96.

After what seems like a very long walk, you make it up to the fence.

Among the scattered sheep, you scan the horizon for signs of human life. You hear a faint shout and turn to see the most wonderful sight: two people on horseback, waving at you!

Not before long, you're in a warm farmhouse, eating a hot meal and trying out your Spanish. Soon, you're reunited with your friends.

Your mountain adventure is over, and you're safe at last.

The end.

The People of the Andes

People have lived in the Andes for thousands of years. The Yaghan people, for example, have lived in Tierra del Fuego (see below) for more than 10,000 years. As in the rest of South America, most of the indigenous people eventually mixed with the settlers from Europe. There is one Yaghan woman who is the last Yahgan person alive. Most people speak Spanish now, but a few still speak the Yaghan language. Tierra del Fuego ('Land of Fire') was named because of the fires of the Yaghan people, which were spotted by the explorer Magellan's expedition around the world.

Further north, people live high up in the Andes mountains. In the Bolivian and Peruvian Andes, the Incas ruled the largest empire in the Americas before the arrival of Europeans. Today, the highest capital city in the world is La Paz in Bolivia, which is 3,640 metres high. Living at high altitudes is physically demanding because there's a shortage of oxygen, and people have had to adapt to living there.

The biggest group of native South American Indians are the Mapuche, most of whom live in Chile today. They fiercely resisted the Spanish conquerors from the 1500s to the 1700s. In the 1800s, the Chilean government settled the Mapuche people on reservations.

Most of the people who live in the rural Andes farm sheep, goats, llamas and alpacas. There are also mines in the Andes, because of its deposits of coal, iron, silver, gold, tin and copper. One of the world's biggest gold mines is in the Andes: Yanacocha in Peru.

In 1865, around 150 Welsh people landed in Patagonia and established Argentina's first Welsh colony, and today there are more than a thousand Welsh speakers in Patagonia.

Amazing Andes Animals

As well as the animals you've already met in this book (pumas, Patagonian foxes, cavies, chinchillas, guanacos, South Andean deer, Andean condors and rheas), the Andes is home to other incredible creatures. They include . . .

- Vizcachas are some of the world's cutest animals. They look like especially furry grey rabbits with long tails, but in fact they're related to chinchillas. They live in dry, desert environments high in the Andes, where they build vast networks of burrows. A different type of vizcacha lives in the plains of Argentina.

- Darwin's frogs are found in Chile and Argentina. They're brown or green with a long snout, and they're unusual because the males incubate eggs inside their mouths. After three weeks, fully formed froglets pop out. The creatures were first classified by Charles Darwin.

- Spectacled bears, the only bear in South America, live in the remote cloud-forests of the Andes, as high in the mountains as 4,300 metres. They're brown or black, usually with white-ish coloured circles around their eyes, which is how they got their name. Male spectacled bears grow up to about 1.8 metres and about 150 kilograms. They're mainly vegetarian, but do sometimes eat meat.

- The yellow tailed woolly monkey is found only in the Andes mountains in Peru. It was thought to be extinct until it was rediscovered in 1974, and today it's still very rare.

Real-life Lost in the Andes Stories

People really have ended up lost in the Andes, with horrifying consequences.

In 1972, a small plane carrying a Uruguayan rugby team from Argentina to Chile crashed in the Andes. The crash, plus an avalanche caused by the crash, left 26 of the 45 passengers and crew dead. The survivors had hardly any food, and the plane had crashed at 11,800 feet. They had a radio to listen to, but no means of signalling, and after 11 days they heard the news that the search for their plane had been given up. They resorted to eating some of the dead, whose bodies were preserved in the snow. Eventually, two of the survivors set off to find help, and came across a remote farmhouse after a gruelling ten-day trek. At the end of the ordeal, after 72 days on the mountain, there were 16 survivors.

Joe Simpson and Simon Yates were climbing Siula Grande, a mountain in Peru in 1985. On the way back down the mountain, Simpson slipped and fell, breaking his leg. His friend was trying to lower him down the mountain when he was forced to cut the rope during a raging storm in order to save himself. Simpson fell 50 metres but survived, and both he and Yates made it back to safety. Simpson wrote a book about their story, which was later made into a film called Touching the Void.

Glossary

agile able to move quickly and easily

altitude sickness illness caused by the lack of oxygen when at high altitude

avalanche rapid fall of snow down a sloping surface

canopy cover formed by a tree's branches

carabiner a metal ring and clip used for fastening ropes when climbing

carrion dead animals

cerebral oedema build-up of fluid around the brain

chinchilla type of rodent with a very soft, grey coat

condor type of vulture; one of the largest flying birds

contaminated unclean

crampons plates with spikes that attach to your shoes so you can walk on ice

crevasse deep, open crack in a glacier or ice sheet

destabilise weaken

dysentery an infection causing diarrhoea

extinct no longer existing

geyser hot spring that sends spouts of hot water and steam into the air

glacier large body of thick ice that is constantly moving

granite grainy type of rock

guanaco animal similar to a llama or alpaca

hypothermia having an abnormally low body temperature

incubate keep eggs warm until they hatch, usually by sitting on them

kindling small, dry twigs used for lighting a fire that will burn quickly and easily

meltwater water released by the melting of snow or ice

oedema swelling in the body caused by build-up of fluid

opportunistic taking advantage of opportunities as they arise

parasite creature that lives in or on another creature

plain broad expanse of flat land

precipice very steep rock face or cliff

pulmonary oedema build-up of fluid around the lungs

puma large, powerful cat

salvaged rescued

scavenge feeding on dead animals or plants

sheer very steep

southern hemisphere parts of the Earth that lie south of the Equator

tectonic plates large slabs of rock that make up the Earth's surface

temperate mild climate

terminus end of an area of ice

terrain physical features of land

tinder very dry material that is easy to set on fire

transceiver device that gives out a signal to indicate where someone is

vicuna animal similar to a llama or alpaca

volcanic fissure crack or vent through which lava erupts

Index

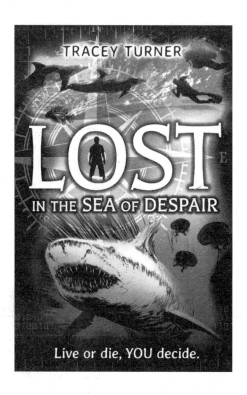

Lost… In the Sea of Despair

You've managed to survive the unpredictable Andes Mountains landscape, but have you got what it takes to survive the vast and perilous Pacific Ocean? From hungry hammerhead sharks to terrifying crashing waves, can you make it out alive?

Surrounded from every angle by the seemingly endless Pacific Ocean, danger can creep up on you from every direction. Will you be able to find your way to safety and avoid becoming a victim of the powerful Pacific waves?

Live or die – you decide.

£4.99   ISBN 9781472906229

Every so often, you peer outside of the raft. The menacing, unmistakable shapes are still there. There are more of them than you thought – you count nine. You decide not to look, and try to concentrate instead on a game of patience with your pack of cards, hoping that the creatures will get bored and go away.

Eventually, after an hour or two worrying about the hammerheads, you risk another look into the sea. They've gone! They must have caught the scent of something more interesting in the water. (To find out more about hammerhead sharks, go to page 19.)

You're starting to wonder when you'll spot another yacht or a ship, or maybe even an island. You unzip the raft and take a good look around. The sun is shining in a clear blue sky – no sign of a plane. Suddenly a dark shape in the water catches your eye. You very much wish it hadn't. It's huge – a three-metre-long creature, just a few metres below the surface and ten or so metres away from the raft. As the raft moves, blown by the wind and pushed by currents, the creature moves with it. You can clearly see by its shape that the creature is a huge shark, with a rounded, white-tipped dorsal fin, and it's following you.

Go to page 43.